aret. Tempest.

Little Grey Rabbit Goes to the Sea was first published
in Great Britain by William Collins Sons & Co 1954

This edition published by HarperCollins*Publishers* 2000
Abridged text copyright © The Alison Uttley Literary Property Trust 2000
Illustrations copyright © The Estate of Margaret Tempest 2000
Copyright this arrangement © HarperCollins*Publishers* 2000
Additional illustration by Mark Burgess
Little Grey Rabbit ® and the Little Grey Rabbit logo are
trademarks of HarperCollins*Publishers* Limited

1 3 5 7 9 10 8 6 4 2

ISBN: 000 198393-8

The HarperCollins website address is: www.**fire**and**water**.com

Printed and bound in Singapore

LITTLE GREY RABBIT
GOES TO THE SEA

ALISON UTTLEY
Pictures by Margaret Tempest

Collins

An Imprint of HarperCollins*Publishers*

SQUIRREL HAD A COLD, Hare had a
cough and Grey Rabbit had the sneezes.
It was all because Hare lost the key of the house
one rainy night.

Grey Rabbit went to visit Mrs Hedgehog and
Squirrel was left at home with Hare to take
care of the house
"Let's go out too, Squirrel," pleaded
Hare. "There are moonshadows and
mushrooms and moldy warps all
over the place. We shall get back
home before Grey Rabbit."

"Lock the door and take the key," said Squirrel, and they ran away together, skipping under the cloudy sky, dancing in the fairy circles.

But the rain came down and Squirrel's tail was soon soaked, and Hare's fur was bedraggled. They were both wet and shivering.

When they got home Grey Rabbit was waiting on the doorstep.

"A-tishoo!" said she.

"A-tishoo!" replied Hare and Squirrel.

"I think I've got a cold," said Grey Rabbit.

"I've got a cold too," said Squirrel. "A-tishoo!"

"I've got two colds," boasted Hare. "A-tishoo! A-tishoo!"

"Where's the key?" asked Grey Rabbit.

Hare felt in his pockets, he picked up the doormat, but there was nothing. They all hunted in the pouring rain, until at last Grey Rabbit found the little key by the garden gate.

How wet they were! Next morning they all had sore throats and bad colds.

"My missus will come over and look after you," said Milkman Hedgehog when Grey Rabbit sneezed on the doorstep.

So they all stayed in bed and Mrs Hedgehog came to nurse them.

They drank coltsfoot tea and sucked butterscotch. Little Fuzzypeg came with a bucket of soup. Mole sent a bunch of fragrant wild thyme. Water Rat brought a pot of lily-bud jam, and Speckledy Hen sent three eggs.

"What they want is a change of air," muttered poor Mrs Hedgehog as she trotted about.

Moldy Warp agreed with her.

"Come and stay underground with me," he invited them. "Nice dark damp house."

"Your house is too stuffy," said Hare, rudely.

"Dear Moldy Warp," said Grey Rabbit. "Your house is very nice, but we are used to sunshine."

"Change of air," advised Water Rat. "Come and live on the river and swim every day with me."

"Oh no," shivered Squirrel. "Too wet."

Wise Owl flew over one night and heard the sneezes.

"What's all this a-tishooing?" he asked. "Squirrel, Hare and Grey Rabbit all got colds? They ought to have a day at the sea."

Nobody answered, but the little animals were listening.

"Too-whit! Too-whee! The beautiful sea," hooted Wise Owl, and he flew away.

"What is the sea?" asked Hare the next day.

Squirrel and Grey Rabbit were not sure, but Fuzzypeg knew, for he went to school.

"It's water. Lots of water," said he. "The sea is salt."

"I don't like water," grumbled Hare. "Or salt."

Grey Rabbit put on her cloak that evening and went to ask Wise Owl about colds and sneezes.

"A day at the sea," advised Wise Owl.

"Where is the sea?" asked Grey Rabbit, but Wise Owl flew into his bedroom chuckling and hooting:

> *"You'll get rid of your sneezes*
> *When you feel the sea breezes.*
> *Too-whit! Too-whee!*
> *The beautiful sea."*

"Silly Old Owl," exclaimed Squirrel, sneezing again.

Moldy Warp was more helpful when Grey Rabbit asked his advice.

"There's a blue caravan on the common," said he. "It belongs to a brown horse, called Duke and a gipsy man. Duke will take you to the sea."

"But-but who will drive?" asked Hare.

"Can't you drive a horse, Hare?" asked Mole. "Just hold the reins and sing out 'Gee-up, Duke.'"

So Hare ran to all his special friends to invite them to go to the sea in a caravan.

Mr and Mrs Hedgehog accepted at once, and Fuzzypeg clapped his paws. Water Rat said he would be delighted, and even the Mole and the Speckledy Hen decided to go.

Everybody got ready. Squirrel made a little tent and Grey Rabbit packed a hamper of food. Hare fetched a spade and bucket. Moldy Warp put a golden guinea in his pocket.

The next morning, as soon as the sun rose, the three little animals set off. "A-tishoo. A-tishoo. A-tishoo!" they sneezed, as they ran over the

fields to the common. The Hedgehog family
waited by the caravan, with Water Rat and the
Speckledy Hen and Moldy Warp.

The old horse showed them the key and they unlocked the door of the caravan. Then with Hare and Moldy Warp and Squirrel on the front seat, and the rest of the animals inside, they started.

"Gee-up!" cried Hare, shaking the reins.

Inside the caravan Grey Rabbit, with the
Hedgehog family, Water Rat and Speckledy Hen,
explored. They jumped on the bed, and looked in
the mirror. Grey Rabbit made a cup of tea and
they ate a few crumbs of biscuit.

The caravan went through villages, past farms
and cottages, down leafy lanes, in the quiet dawn.
The horse chose the byways where they met
nobody except a few wandering animals.

After a time everyone fell asleep, rocked by the
motion of the swinging caravan. The old horse
jogged along peacefully, for he knew every step of
the way. He came at last to a lane which led to
the grassy top of the cliffs, and at the end of this
green path he stopped.

"Here we are," he neighed.

Hare tumbled off his seat down to the grass, and with him fell Squirrel and Mole, who were wrapped in the rug.

"The sea! The glorious sea!" shouted Hare, dancing to the door of the caravan.

Grey Rabbit and the others hurried out, laughing and cheering as they saw the wide green sea with the little snowy waves, curling in the distance.

"Unharness me," said Duke, turning his head. "There's a sandy cove below the cliffs. Go and enjoy yourselves and come back when the sun goes down to bathe."

They collected their belongings and ran down the narrow track to the sea.

When they reached the bottom they all gave little shrieks of joy. They felt the warm sand under their feet, and the strong sea air in their fur and feathers.

They stood looking at the vast stretch of water, and they saw the little curling waves, each edged with white lace like Grey Rabbit's best petticoat.

"What does the sea talk about?" asked Fuzzypeg, holding tight to Grey Rabbit's hand. He was rather frightened by the little waves that rolled up to his feet.

"Sea breezes. Sea breezes. No more of your sneezes," whispered the sea.

Hare picked up a strand of seaweed, but the waves came up and washed his feet. With a wild cry he ran away, but when he looked round the sea also had turned back.

"It keeps coming and going," said he, puzzled.

There were several strangers on the beach. A flock of snowy seagulls walked on the sand, and

a black cormorant sat fishing from a rock.

"Grey Rabbit, Grey Rabbit," sang the little curling waves as they lapped at Grey Rabbit's soft little feet, and touched her grey dress.

The sea wind blew her apron like a sail, and
tugged at her petticoat. It pulled Hare's red coat,
and ruffled Squirrel's tail. It nipped Mr Hedgehog's

nose, and tossed Fuzzypeg's smock over his head.

"Wise Owl said the sea would take our tishoos away, but I'm going to sneeze," announced Grey Rabbit. Hare and Squirrel both wrinkled up their noses, as they felt a sneeze coming.

"A-tishoo! A-tishoo! A-tishoo!" they all sneezed together.

The breeze caught those sneezes and tossed them up in the air. They floated away like baby clouds in the blue sky.

"My tishoo has gone," cried Grey Rabbit. "I'm quite well! Hurray!"

"Mine's gone too," added Squirrel.

"Hurray! Both my tishoos have flown away!" laughed Hare, and the three animals danced on the sand, waving their paws.

Then Grey Rabbit lifted up her grey skirt and paddled in the sea. Fuzzypeg joined her. He was so small a wave might have upset him, so he held tight to her apron.

Water Rat took off his velvet coat and white ruffles and swam in the shallow water. Hare plucked up his courage, took off his red coat and rushed into the sea, and then out again, as he saw a wave coming.

Squirrel, with a cockleshell tied on her head for a hat and a garland of seaweed round her neck, began to dance on the edge of the sea, and Moldy Warp dug a tunnel and made a mole heap.

Suddenly there was a shout from the Hedgehogs. And the Speckledy Hen cackled from her nest of pebbles.

"Thief! Robber! Bandit!" they called.

A seagull flew away with Hare's red coat and a second gull took Water Rat's frills. The birds flew to a rocky part of the cliff, where they dropped their treasures by their nests, with loud squawks to their wives and babies.

"Fine bedcovers," they cried.

The group of little animals on the beach could see the red coat and white ruffles hanging far above them on the wild rocky cliff.

"Who is going to get them back?" asked Hare, dancing with rage.

"I'll go," said Grey Rabbit.

"And I," added Squirrel.

"Then I'll go and take care of you," said Hare.

So the three little animals climbed the high dangerous rocks, and Squirrel on her nimble feet was always the first. She swung up the gorse bushes, and skipped over the cracks. Hare leapt up and down, rushing forward and then stopping in alarm. Grey Rabbit plodded silently along behind them. Squirrel arrived first at the ledge where the seagulls' nests lay.

Little grey gulls were toddling about, but when
Squirrel came near the mother gulls pecked
fiercely at her head. Luckily Squirrel wore the
cockleshell hat she had picked up on the beach,
and this protected her.

"Oh! Oh!" screamed the gulls.
"You have a very hard head."

"I want Hare's coat and Water Rat's frills," said
Squirrel, trembling with fright.

Then Hare's head popped round the corner and
Grey Rabbit's startled little face appeared.

The gulls swooped at them, but Grey Rabbit shook her apron in their faces, and Hare gave a queer shrill cry, remarkably like Wise Owl's call,

"Too-whit! Too-whee-ee-ee!

The horrible sea!" he hooted.

The noise frightened the gulls away for a moment, and the three seized the red coat and the torn snowy frills, and ran off, tumbling, rolling, tearing their fur, scratching their legs, as they fell down the cliff to their friends at the bottom.

"Never make friends with a wild seagull," said Fuzzypeg solemnly.

Hare put on his coat. Squirrel combed her tail. Grey Rabbit pulled thorns from her fur and bathed her cut feet.

Mrs Hedgehog lighted a fire of driftwood, and
they filled the kettle from a stream that ran down
the rocks.

Then, with the bright fire crackling, and the good
tea brewing, and the food spread out, they
enjoyed the picnic and forgot their troubles.

"Now for a sand pie," said Hare, when all the
food was eaten. He filled his bucket with sand,
and the rest watched, for Hare was sometimes
very clever at doing things. He patted the top firm,
and turned it upside down. He looked round at his
audience, and then he slowly lifted the bucket.

There was a lovely golden pie, as nice to look at
as Grey Rabbit's sponge pudding!

They all had a taste, but nobody liked it very much. Hare was so proud of his first pie he made another and another, until he had a ring of them. Squirrel put a cockleshell on each turret, Grey Rabbit draped seaweed about them, and little Fuzzypeg found pebbles to adorn them.

Hare leapt over them, and Fuzzypeg followed, crying "Follow my leader," but nobody could jump high like Hare.

They wandered along the sandy strip, and all was quiet except for the music of the waves. They found beautiful pebbles, and pearly shells. Grey Rabbit picked up a starfish and Squirrel found a mermaid's purse.

Hare found a long razor-shell, Fuzzypeg gathered a lot of seaweed balloons, and Water Rat discovered a sea urchin, prickly as Mr Hedgehog himself.

So the happy day passed, and the sun moved down to the sea to bathe in a flood of gold.

"What time is it, Hare?" asked Grey Rabbit.

Hare looked at his watch. The fingers pointed as usual to twelve o'clock. The watch had not kept time since Hare once stirred his tea with it. He dipped the watch in the sea and listened.

"Tick Tack, time to go back," said the fat little watch, and the fingers began to move again.

"The sea has cured my watch too," cried Hare.

They put the starfish in the bucket which they
half filled with water, so that the tide
would not flow over the edge.

They twined seaweed round their
necks, and stuffed their pockets with
striped pebbles. Then, waving goodbye
to the sea, they wandered wearily up the steep
narrow track.

"Hurry up," cried Duke, who was expecting
them. "The sun is getting into the sea."

Far away they saw a golden track on the water,
like a pathway in the waves.

Hare fastened the horse's traces, and clambered
inside the caravan.

Everyone got into the bed, and nobody bothered
to drive.

The horse jogged along the lanes, and the first
stars pricked the evening sky. Inside the caravan
all was quiet, for every little animal was fast asleep.

They reached the common at midnight without
any more adventures, and, yawning, they tumbled
out on the grass. Grey Rabbit locked the door
and Hare unharnessed the horse.

The gipsy lay under a bush
wrapped in a coat, snoring, so
after whispering their thanks
to Duke they all hurried away.

The Speckledy Hen flew over the fields.

Moldy Warp went underground to his home.

Water Rat ran swiftly to the river.

Mr and Mrs Hedgehog with a sleepy little Fuzzypeg went slowly to the cottage.

Squirrel, Hare and little Grey Rabbit ran along the field paths, with many a backward look.

They found their key, and entered the house, and went to bed.

"Seabreezes. Seabreezes," murmured Grey Rabbit, as she curled up under the blanket. "I like the seabreezes."

In the morning the gipsy opened his eyes and stared at the caravan. He unlocked the door and looked suspiciously around. A necklace of seaweed hung from a hook, a heap of shells lay on the rumpled bed. Little footprints were everywhere. In a mug was a golden guinea.

"Real gold," said he, biting it. "Now I wonder who took this caravan!"

Duke never said a word. He went on nibbling the grass, and laughing softly to himself over the adventure.